Dear Old Dumpling

Illustrated by Pierre-André Derome
Translated by Sarah Cummins

First Novels

Formac Publishing Company Limited
Halifax
2002

Originally published as *Mon cher Chausson*

Formac Publishing Company Limited acknowledges the support
of the Cultural Affairs Section, Nova Scotia Department of
Tourism and Culture. We acknowledge the financial support of the
Government of Canada through the Book Publishing Industry
Development Program (BPIDP) for our publishing activities.

We acknowledge the support of the Canada Council for the Arts
for our publishing program.

National Library of Canada Cataloguing in Publication Data

Gauthier, Gilles, 1943-
[Mon cher Chausson. English]
    Dear old Dumpling / Gilles Gauthier; illustrated by
    Pierre-André Derome.

(First novels; #42)
Translation of: Mon cher Chausson.
ISBN 0-88780-574-4 (pbk.).—ISBN 0-88780-575-2 (hdc.)

    I. Derome, Pierre-André, 1952- II. Title.
    III. Title: Mon cher Chausson. English. IV. Series.

PS8563.A858M6613 2002   jC843'.54   C2002-903305-5
PQ3919.2.G3794M6613 2002

Formac Publishing Company Limited
5502 Atlantic Street
Halifax, Nova Scotia B3H 1G4
www.formac.ca

Printed and bound in Canada

Distributed in the United States by:
Orca Book Publishers
P.O. Box 468 Custer, WA
USA 98240-0468

Distributed in the UK by:
Roundabout Books (a division of
Roundhouse Publishing Ltd.)
31 Oakdale Glen, Harrogate,
N Yorkshire. HG1 2YJ

Table of Contents

1
Dumpling Goes Wild

Gary and I couldn't figure it out. For several days, Dumpling just hadn't been himself. We couldn't control him.

Our little puppy, once afraid of his own shadow, seemed to think he was a lion. He tried to catch every sparrow he saw and chased squirrels out of the yard. He had turned into a real terror!

He even made our neighbours' big tomcat Smoky turn tail. In all her life, Mooch had never managed to

do that! And she was a
German shepherd!

Gary's dad Jack noticed the
change too. He couldn't let
Dumpling out on Tuesdays and
Fridays anymore. Dumpling

kept barking at the garbage truck. He was defending his garbage cans!

The only person who didn't seem surprised was my mom, Judy. She said she had a pretty good idea about what had brought about this change in Dumpling. But she was keeping us all in the dark.

She did promise she would finally tell us when Gary and Dumpling came over after school. Jack would be there too. He always came over to chat with my mom. So we would finally find out the big secret.

So there we all were, sitting around the table, looking expectantly at Judy. She observed Dumpling with an

amused look on her face. She was going to make us beg.

"Come on, Mom, tell us! What's your explanation?"

"I'm hesitant to tell you the truth, Carl. I don't know how you'll react."

"It's not something bad, is it? Dumpling doesn't have rabies or anything, does he?"

Judy smiled. "No, he doesn't have rabies, but—"

I felt the blood drain from my face. Gary looked

stricken. Judy quickly reassured him.

"Dumpling isn't sick. In fact, he's in great shape."

Relief spread over Gary's face.

"Then why is he acting so strange?"

Judy seemed to be considering the question.

"Maybe you won't believe me," she said in a serious voice, "but our little Dumpling is in love!"

Gary and I had expected anything but that! We both turned and looked at Dumpling and burst out laughing.

"Dumpling? In love?"

Gary was wriggling with mirth, and I was laughing so

hard I could hardly catch my breath. When I had calmed down a bit, I turned to Judy.

"I suppose he's in love with a German shepherd?" I joked.

Gary and I burst out laughing again, but Judy just stared at me, open-mouthed.

Then she asked, in a puzzled tone, "How did you know?"

2
The Mysterious German Shepherd

Once Judy revealed Dumpling's great secret to us, Gary and I had only one thing in mind: we wanted to meet the sorceress who had cast a spell on Dumpling.

The first time she showed up, Gary and I were out with Jack, running errands. Mom had never seen this dog before. She thought it was a stray.

The dog wore no collar and was pretty skinny. She came into the yard and danced around Dumpling, trying to get him to play.

When they finally stopped chasing one another, Dumpling's tongue was hanging out and he was panting. The other dog rested a little while, then went away. Dumpling watched her go and stared in the same direction for a long time.

And that is when the change in Dumpling first began. He leapt up and took off like a race car after some young squirrel he had glimpsed from the corner of his eye.

Dumpling went wild. He tried to climb the tree where the squirrel had taken refuge. He stood against the trunk, scratching the bark with his claws.

Mom was worried about
making me unhappy and
decided not to say anything to
us when we got back. She
thought the German shepherd
would remind me of Mooch.

She figured Dumpling would soon return to normal.

But when that didn't happen, she decided to tell us. And now it was time to track down this other dog.

Gary and I couldn't let the story end there. We had to see this famous German shepherd with our own eyes, so we came up with a plan.

We would let Dumpling lead us to her. If he really was in love, he would be anxious to find his sweetheart. If we let him go wherever he wanted, he would lead us straight to her lair.

But our plan was a total failure. Dumpling seemed to delight in leading us on a wild goose chase. After an hour,

we had made the acquaintance of a hideous bulldog, an insignificant chihuahua, a horse and a rabbit.

Either Dumpling's nose was stuffed up and he had no sense of smell, or else he didn't want to reveal his girlfriend's hiding place. We needed reinforcements!

We decided to go back home and ask Jack for help. We might have better luck if we drove through the neighbourhood. If that dog was anywhere around, we should be able to spot her.

We obviously couldn't count on our furry sleuth!

3
A Surprising Sight

Our trio returned home disappointed. Dumpling trailed behind Gary and me, his nose to the ground. In silence, we climbed the stairs leading to the balcony.

As he passed in front of the kitchen window, Gary glanced inside. He stopped short and beckoned to me to come over without making any noise. We stood at the window, transfixed.

My mom and Gary's dad were kissing. They hadn't heard us coming. They must have thought we were still

miles away. Jack was stroking Judy's hair tenderly.

We stepped back from the window, and I pointed to the shed. Gary understood that I wanted to talk to him. We tiptoed back down to the yard.

Unfortunately, we had forgotten about Dumpling.

Instead of following us, Dumpling dashed toward the house. He started to howl like a lost puppy. Five seconds later, Judy and Jack came outside.

They should have been blushing and embarrassed when they saw us. But in fact, we were the embarrassed ones. We felt like two prowlers caught red-handed.

Gary was the first to recover his poise.

"We couldn't find the dog," he started to explain. "So we thought we'd look closer to home."

I tried to help him out.

"Maybe she's hiding behind the shed. Or in the woods over there."

Jack and Judy just looked at us. They didn't seem convinced by our lame explanations.

"That dog must be far away by now," Judy said. "If she were around here, Dumpling would know it."

Given Dumpling's previous failure as a bloodhound, I wasn't so sure.

"Dumpling is young and inexperienced," I answered. "You can't really rely on him."

"Dogs are born with a heightened sense of smell," Jack put in. "It's innate."

"There must be exceptions," Gary said, taking my side. "There must be some dogs

that are born with no sense of smell."

Jack picked up Dumpling. "If this dog had no sense of smell, he wouldn't always be poking his nose in the fridge."

Dumpling wagged his tail and tried to lick Jack's face, as if he was grateful to have at least one defender.

I decided it was best to

leave Jack to his illusions. I turned the conversation toward our plan to continue the search.

"The German shepherd must have covered a lot of ground since Mom saw her. We need to look for her in a car. If that's not too much trouble?"

As I spoke, I was sure that Jack and Judy would know we had seen them kissing, but I don't think they suspected a thing.

Jack took out his car keys and skipped downstairs. He opened the car door like a limousine driver.

"Come along, Dumpling. We're going to find your lady-love."

A little smile flitted across Judy's face.

4
One Lost, Three Found

The mysterious German shepherd remained hidden. We scoured the neighbourhood, yet found not a trace of our visitor. Judy called the dog pound, but to no avail.

I figured that poor Dumpling would have to forget about her. He would have to find another girlfriend or remain a bachelor. He is still young. He has his whole life ahead of him.

The same can't be said for Jack and Judy.

Gary and I had a long talk

about this. Both of us knew
that our parents were getting
along very well. But now we
realized that there was more
to it.

Before, I could never

imagine my mother with another man. Even though my father had died several years ago, I couldn't believe that she would want to find someone new.

When Jack first got interested in Judy, I didn't like it one bit. I was really jealous. But, as I told Gary, my feelings have changed since then.

My mom doesn't have to live alone for the rest of her life. She's entitled to fall in love again. And if there's going to be a new man in her life, I'd just as soon it was Jack.

He takes care of Gary. He gave him Dumpling. And I have to say he's always been

very nice to me.

Gary admitted that he too had been jealous. His mother died when Gary was born. He never wanted another mother. But now he's beginning to think he could make an exception for Judy.

Gary thinks she is gentle and kind, and she has helped his dad a lot. With Judy, Jack seems more at ease with himself. He's more affectionate.

As for Gary and me, there's no problem. Gary is my best friend and he always will be. Sometimes we fight, but no more than real brothers.

And another thing: since Mooch died, we now have Dumpling in common!

5
The Book of Mooch

Even though I'm glad Dumpling is around, I still miss Mooch a lot.

Judy was right when she hesitated to tell me about the German shepherd. All the time we were searching the neighbourhood, it was Mooch I was looking for. I know that sounds ridiculous.

I couldn't keep myself from dreaming that Mooch had come back, that she had conquered death and come back home.

I told myself that Mooch

was wondering how I was getting along without her. She had come back to help Dumpling grow up into a real dog. I was terribly disappointed when our search was unsuccessful.

To cheer myself up, I worked on my biography of Mooch. That was one way I could be with my dear friend again. With every sentence I wrote about her, I brought her back to life a little bit.

When I wrote about the sad parts, I started to cry. Other times, I laughed out loud over the crazy things we did.

I can just picture it: Mooch reeking of skunk perfume while I tried to get her into a tomato-juice bath!

6
A Sticky Situation

You'll never guess what happened. Dumpling disguised himself as a skunk. I suppose he was trying to attract his German shepherd.

It happened yesterday, when Gary and I were making one last attempt to track down the missing dog. We were looking in the woods behind Gary's house, and we thought Dumpling was with us.

But, as is his wont these days, Sir Dumpling was exploring the wider world. He had gradually gone farther and farther away from us. He must have been enjoying playing king of the forest.

Dumpling probably decided to chase an innocent squirrel. Maybe he saw one on the other side of the street. He just headed straight that way, without looking where he was stepping.

City workers had been doing some road-work in the area, and the street was full of fresh tar. Dumpling discovered this the hard way.

He tried to stop and go back the way he had come, but he fell flat on his belly in the sticky black goo.

When he finally extricated himself from the tar, he decided to clean it off. So he went and

rolled in some leaves.

When he came back to find us, Dumpling looked like he was ready for Halloween. Have you ever seen a skunk dressed in camouflage?

We picked him up and, holding him as far away from us as our arms would stretch, we carried him home. Judy was astounded when she saw this beast. She thought we had discovered a new species!

Jack burst out laughing. He said it was the first time he had seen a four-legged walking shrub. He thought it was pretty funny to be cleaning up a shrub.

Tar is incredibly sticky. It was hard to remove it without scalping poor Dumpling. We couldn't use anything that might burn his skin.

After two hours of rub-a-dub-shrub, Dumpling was finally presentable again. He had more black on him than before, but at least he wasn't

sticky. We were certain that he had learned his lesson.

How wrong we were!

7
Do Moles Bark?

That German shepherd had certainly made Dumpling lose his head. Just two days after the tar incident, Dumpling went walkabout again. And this time he didn't come back.

Dear old Dumpling decided to play hide-and-go-seek. We never figured out how he managed to slip down a rabbit hole, but the spelunker had been trapped down there for half an hour already.

We could hear him barking underground, but he had no idea how to come back up.

He was all alone and lost in the dark. Maybe the tunnel had collapsed on him.

One thing was certain: Dumpling was in serious trouble, and so were we. None of us knew what to do.

Jack was worried about digging. He was afraid the ground would collapse on Dumpling. Gary was beside himself and couldn't stop yelling. Judy tried to calm him down.

Suddenly, the barking stopped. Not a sound came from the hole.

Jack stared at Judy in silence. They both looked stricken. Gary was about to panic.

"Quick, Dad! We've got to

do something. Dumpling is suffocating! You can't let him die!"

Judy went over to him.

"Dumpling was barking for twenty minutes. That must have tired him out, and he's catching his breath."

Gary looked at his dad. He didn't seem to be convinced.

"Do you really think Dumpling's resting, Dad?"

"He must be looking hard for another way out."

Gary's eyes filled with tears. I tried to cheer him up.

"Remember Mooch was always getting lost. But she always came back."

"But Mooch was a German shepherd. Dumpling's just a little puppy."

I didn't know what to say. It's true that Dumpling isn't very—

"Something just moved!"

It was Jack who spoke. His head was almost inside the hole.

"Yes! I'm sure the noise is getting louder. Come on, Dumpling. Come on, boy. You can do it!"

Gary ran over to his dad.

"Don't give up, Dumpling.

We're here. We'll never scold you again, Dumpling, I promise. Come on, Dumpling."

Then the noise stopped. Gary and Jack didn't move. Judy lowered her eyes.

Then, fortunately, the noises started up again.

"That's right, doggie. Take it easy. Come on, come toward the light. It's great up here."

Gary was full of confidence now. We could hear panting. Dumpling must be near.

And he was! Jack saw him at the bottom of the hole.

"That's right, Dumpling. Come along."

Finally, Dumpling was safe! Gary held him in his arms and smothered him with kisses. His lips were all covered in dirt.

Dumpling had something in his mouth. Could it be...? It seemed impossible, but yes! I was sure it was.

Mooch's old red-white-and-blue ball! The one my dad had bought. We used to throw it for Mooch to fetch.

Mooch's ball had come back.

8
Life's Relay Race

I sat on the bed with the ball in front of me. The old chewed-up ball that belonged to Mooch. I couldn't take my eyes off it.

When Judy saw it the other day, she turned pale. I was sure she was thinking about Dad as she held it in the palm of her hand.

Then she gave it back to me. I checked that it really was Mooch's old ball. I was sure it was.

Jack claimed that this proved what a good sniffer

dog Dumpling was. Despite
how long it had been
underground, Dumpling was
still able to track its scent.

Gary agreed with his dad.
He was really proud of

Dumpling and thought he was
amazing. But I had my own
version of the facts.

When Judy and I were alone,
I told her what I thought.

"I think that Dumpling had

help from your famous German shepherd. That dog was a messenger."

"A messenger?"

"A messenger from Mooch. Mooch wanted to let me know she hadn't forgotten me."

Judy's eyes were glistening. I finished my version of the story.

"Mooch left me a souvenir. And your strange German shepherd told Dumpling where to look."

Mom sat down beside me and hugged me close. Then she placed the ball in my hand.

"Mooch passed us this ball, like in a relay race. She has run her leg in the race of life. Now she wants us to run ours."

I nodded, then I reached under the bed and pulled out the spiral notebook in which I had written my book about Mooch. I handed it to Judy.

"I've finished her biography."

9
A Five-star Night

One evening when we were out looking at the sky, Jack started chuckling softly.

"Did you two know that each of your dogs has its own star? Sirius is the star of Canis Major, the big dog. And Procyon is the star of Canis Minor, the little dog."

Gary and I thought that Jack was kidding us. But at school we looked through a big book about astronomy. To our astonishment, we found out that Jack was telling the truth.

Since then, two stars in our own personal sky have changed their names. Sirius is now called Mooch, and Procyon is called Dumpling.

And tonight, our own little Canis Minor will become a star on earth.

Today Dumpling turns one year old. Gary and I decided to have a candle-lit celebration. Our parents prepared the food, and we took care of the presents.

Since Dumpling likes chocolate, we bought a tin of cookies. We wrapped it up in silver paper. Dumpling's going to love it.

To help Dumpling keep in shape after all those cookies, we got a ball. It looks like

Mooch's ball, but it's sturdier. Now the squirrels can relax.

And, just for fun, we made a crown. Dumpling is the king of the party, and we will crown him Dumpling the First.

Judy placed a cake with one candle on the table. The future king had to blow out the candle.

But we couldn't keep Dumpling still long enough to blow it out. He was afraid of the flame and just wanted to run away. Jack said we should help him.

We all stood around the candle and blew up a storm. The flame could not resist.

Dumpling was very excited. Gary sat him in a chair and

put the crown on his head. We all began to sing:

Happy birthday to you,
Happy birthday to you
Happy birthday, dear
  Dumpling
Happy birthday to you!

The crown was too big and it slipped down over Dumpling's eyes. Gary started shouting at the top of his voice.
Hip hip hooray!
Hip hip hooray!
He picked up Dumpling and carried him over to Judy.
"The King requires a kiss."
Judy bent over Dumpling, but Dumpling didn't know what she was doing and tried to squirm away. Jack thought

that was hilarious.

"I think the king would prefer to be kissed by a German shepherd."

Judy pretended to be offended.

"Dumpling is too young. He's not used to it."

"You'd better show him how, then," Gary said, looking at his dad with a funny expression. Jack looked startled, and Judy turned bright red, like the colour of her dress.

Gary pushed Jack toward Judy, and I went over to help.

"Come on, Mom, don't be embarrassed. We know that you two have been kissing. We spied on you."

"You admit that!"

"We're not little kids, you know. You don't have to hide!"

Judy just shook her head. Jack sidled over.

"Our secret is out!"

Judy shrugged. She half-closed her eyes. Their lips touched.

Gary grinned. He spoke to the king of the evening.

"You see, Dumpling, it's easy. There's nothing to be afraid of. Now hold still."

Dumpling stared at Gary, mesmerized. Gary bent his lips toward Dumpling.

And then Dumpling licked him on the nose!

Three more new novels in the *First Novels Series*!

Fred's Halloween Adventure
By Marie-Danielle Croteau
Illustrated by Bruno St. Aubin

Fred is going to spend Halloween with his friend William and they are going to be part of the pumpkin festival. William's dad has grown a huge pumpkin. It is so huge that the giant vegetable will travel to the show on a horse-drawn cart. Now Fred finds he has agreed to be Cinderella and travel inside the pumpkin — a trip that turns into a disaster.

Maddie's Millionaire Dreams
By Louise Leblanc
Illustrated by Marie-Louise Gay

Maddie needs some money, enough money to live like a millionaire. Nicholas has a plan to get lottery tickets at his family's grocery store if she will give him the money. The gang soon find out that the lottery can be addictive. They are losing more than they are winning and now Nicholas has to repay money he has taken from the store. That's when Maddie turns her hand to business to help Nicholas and herself.

Marilou Cries Wolf

By Raymond Plante
Illustrated by Marie Claude Favreau

Marilou is bored. Her friends are busy and there's nothing interesting on television. Her dad is repairing an antique radio, so she plays a trick on Boris and then another one on the twins. The police and the fire department arrive to put out a non-existent fire. No one is amused. So they play a trick on Marilou so that she will never, ever cry wolf again.

Meet all the great kids in the *First Novels Series*!

Meet Arthur — an only child with a great Dad
Arthur Throws a Tantrum
Arthur's Dad
Arthur's Problem Puppy

Meet Fred — whose wild imagination and love of cats gets him into all kinds of trouble!
Fred on the Ice Floes
Fred and the Food
Fred and the Stinky Cheese
Fred's Dream Cat
Fred's Midnight Prowler

Meet Maddie — irrepressible Maddie whose family is just too much sometimes
Maddie Needs her Own Life

Meet Marilou — and her clan of clever friends

Meet Mikey — a small boy with a big problem

Meet Mooch — and Carl, who is learning lessons about life thanks to his dog Mooch

---

Formac Publishing Company Limited
5502 Atlantic Street, Halifax, Nova Scotia B3H 1G4
Orders: 1-800-565-1975 Fax: (902) 425-0166
www.formac.ca